by Walter Farley

The famous Walter Farley (whose Black Stallion stories are loved by millions of older children) has now written a story every beginning reader not only *can* but will *want* to read and re-read *all by himself*.

A child who loves ponies will lose his heart to Little Black. Little Black is a little pony who wants *so* much to be big and do the things a big horse can do.

The story is told with warmth and pathos, with charming illustrations by James Schucker.

Little Black, A Pony

By Walter Farley

Illustrated by James Schucker

This book is made possible by a grant from The Bert Martin Foundation.

For Steve, who helped write it.

ISBN 0760721920

Printed and bound in USA

M 9 8 7 6 5 4 3

When I was little I had a
pony. I called him Little
Black. He was my very, very
good friend.

The two of us went all over the farm.

We had fun. We went to see the other horses. We saw Big Red.

My, that horse could run!

Then one day I said, "Little Black, I would like to try to ride Big Red."

So I went to the barn.

I looked at Big Red.

Could I ride this horse?

Could I ride this big horse?

I could!

I could ride Big Red!

It was fun!

All my friends stopped to look at me.

I went by Little Black. But he would not look at me.

Soon I began to jump Big Red. This horse could do everything!

We jumped and jumped.

But when I went by Little
Black, his head was down.
He looked sad.

Then one day I took Big Red out for a long ride.

What a day!

What a time we had!

Little Black came running along right after us.

He could not keep up with us. He tried but he was too little.

He could not run as fast as Big Red.

We went on.

A big tree was down.

It was in the way.

Big Red jumped right over
the tree.

To him it was just a hop!

It was not just a hop to
Little Black.

But he tried it.

He tried to jump over the
tree.

But Little Black could not
jump that high.

Down he went.

His leg was stuck.

It was stuck in the tree.

"Oh, Big Red," I said. "My pony wants so much to do everything you do! Look at him! His leg is stuck. He can't get up!

"We must go back! We must help him! Come on."

I took hold of the tree.

I had to pull, and pull, and pull.

It took a long time.

At last I got his leg out.

Then I talked to Little Black.

"Please don't try to do everything Big Red does. He is a big horse. You are only a little pony. You could get hurt."

I talked and talked to him. I wanted him to be happy.

But he would not look at me.

He just looked sad.

So I was sad, too.

Days went by.

Then I took Big Red out again. Little Black came along too.

But he did not hold his head up.

He did not hold his tail up.

He just looked sad.

We went down to the river.
It was so hot! I sat down
under a tree. Big Red went
into the water. He went way
out. There the water went
very, very fast.

Little Black put two feet into the water.

Was he going to do just what Big Red did?

Was he going out in the fast water, too?

"Come back here, Little Black," I said. "You could get hurt."

I took hold of him. I pulled him back.

"You can't go out there! The water is too fast for you. Don't try to do just what Big Red does! He is a big horse! You are just a little pony."

After that day, Little Black
was more and more sad.

He would not look up when
I went to see him. I guess he
thought he was no good at all.

He did not eat very much.

When I tried to give him
apples, he would not eat them.

This made me very sad.

Little Black was my friend.
I wanted him to be happy.

One morning it was very
cold.

Just as the sun came up, I
looked out.

There was Little Black.

My friend, my good little
pony, was running away.

I had to get him back!

I ran down to the barn and
jumped on Big Red. "Hurry!
Hurry!" I said. "We must go
and get my pony!"

We went out of the barn
fast.

We could see Little Black's
tracks in the snow.

On and on we ran in the
snow. We went right along in the
tracks of Little Black.

But I could not see him.

"Little Black," I called.

"Please come back! I love
you more than any horse!"

Then we came to the river.

The river was all ice!

Big Red did not like the
look of that ice.

He stopped.

"Come on!" I said to Big Red.

"Little Black is over there in the trees! He went over the ice! You can, too! Come on! Try it!"

He did try it!

But the ice did not hold Big Red.

Crack! Splash!

Down I went.

Down I went into the cold water.

Big Red got back up on the
bank.

I tried and tried to get
there too.

But I could not.

My feet were cold.

My hands were cold.

I was cold all over.

"Help! Help!" I called.

But Big Red could not help
me.

47

Then I saw something on
the other bank.

Something in the trees!

It was Little Black.

He saw me in the water.

"Help me, Little Black," I called.

"Help me! You can run on the ice! You are little! The ice will hold you!"

Little Black looked at me.

He looked at the ice.

And then his head went up.

His tail went out.

He was not sad any more.

Here was something he could do!

Little Black came.

He came to me over the ice.

"Come on, boy!" I called.

"You are going to make it."

Little Black got to me.

He let me take hold of his tail.

Then he pulled and pulled to get me out of the water.

Then he pulled and pulled to get me up on the ice.

Would the ice hold the two of us?

The ice did hold us.

And on over the ice we went!

Little Black pulled me back to the bank of the river.

"Good boy," I said. "You saved me!"

Now Little Black put his head up high. My, he was happy! At last he had done something Big Red could not do.

That night all my friends came to see Little Black.

We were all as happy as he. "Little Black," I said, "there is no horse like you. You are the best of all! And I will ride only you from now on."

WALTER FARLEY'S first Beginner Book naturally has to do with horses.

As far back as he can remember they were his first love. When his English professor at Columbia University suggested writing as a career, he was on his way. His fifteen Black Stallion books are now world-famous. Millions of boys and girls aged ten and upwards are such fans that they want to own the whole series.

Mr. Farley is married, and has two girls and two boys. He hopes that all of them will grow up to be enthusiastic horse lovers.

JAMES SCHUCKER has drawn pictures from the day he was given his first pencil. He loves animals — particularly horses. He is married, has one daughter and lives in Quakertown, Pennsylvania.